STEFAN ZWEIG was born in 1881 in Vienna, into a wealthy
Austrian-Jewish family. He studied in Berlin and Vienna
and was first known as a poet and translator, then as a
biographer. Zweig travelled widely, living in Salzburg
between the wars, and was an international bestseller with
a string of hugely popular novellas including *Letter from an
Unknown Woman*, *Amok* and *Fear*. In 1934, with the rise of
Nazism, he moved to London, and later on to Bath, taking
British citizenship after the outbreak of the Second World
War. With the fall of France in 1940 Zweig left Britain for
New York, before settling in Brazil, where in 1942 he and
his wife were found dead in an apparent double suicide.
Much of his work is available from Pushkin Press.

JOURNEY INTO
THE PAST

STEFAN ZWEIG

JOURNEY INTO THE PAST

Translated from the German
and with an afterword by
Anthea Bell

Foreword by
Paul Bailey

PUSHKIN PRESS
LONDON

Pushkin Press
71-75 Shelton Street,
London WC2H 9JQ

English translation and afterword © Anthea Bell 2009
Foreword © Paul Bailey 2009

Journey into the Past first published in German as
Widerstand der Wirklichkeit
© Williams Verlag Zurich 1976

First published by Pushkin Press in 2009

This edition first published in 2013
Reprinted in 2013

ISBN 978 1 908968 36 4

Set in 12 on 16 Baskerville Monotype
Printed and bound by
CPI Group (UK) Ltd, Croydon, CR0 4YY

www.pushkinpress.com

Contents

THE RESURRECTED MASTER

The Subtle Fiction of Stefan Zweig

I T IS ONLY IN RECENT YEARS that Stefan Zweig has been recognised and lauded by English-speaking readers as an incomparable storyteller. His reputation in Britain during the 1920s and 30s was based almost entirely on his short and informative biographies of Marie Antoinette, Casanova, Tolstoy and—among the then living—Romain Rolland and Sigmund Freud, both of whom he had befriended. Rolland, the author of the turgid but worthy novel *Jean-Christophe*, inspired by the life of Beethoven, was awarded the Nobel Prize for Literature in 1916. Rolland, a pacifist and musicologist, kept his imaginative distance from such unsavoury human foibles as envy and spite and downright wickedness—qualities that are explored and dramatized in Thomas Mann's altogether superior fictional study of a great composer *Doctor Faustus*. The kindly, decent Romain Rolland is

9

virtually forgotten today, but Zweig, his eulo-gistic biographer, lives on in the comparatively modest forms of the novella and the short story.

He was capable of writing at greater length, as his most substantial and famous novel, *Beware of Pity* (1939) and the recently translated and published *The Post Office Girl* testify. Yet his heart was in the *conte*—the tale told by word of mouth, or by letter, that can be read at a single sitting. Each of his varied narrators has something urgent to impart—a long-buried secret, the confession of a misdeed, or the revelation of the truth behind a circumstance others had accepted at face value. They are people with a pressing need to make sense of the inexplicable. They question why their lives have gone astray and why they allowed their feelings to override convention and common sense. They are, by and large, victims and survivors of the last days of the Austro-Hungarian Empire and it would be easy to dismiss them as decadent. Zweig puts decadence in perspective, neither revelling in its attractiveness nor castigating its more squalid aspects. It is to his aesthetic purpose to sound the human note, and to do so in such a disarming manner as to shame the reader who has already made facile judgements. His men and women are complicated, and he would not have it otherwise. He is a celebrator of confusion—the word he employs as the title for a brief masterpiece that bears comparison with Mann's *Death in Venice*—and it is in a confused state that they seek to explicate their often banal misfortunes.

Zweig's narrative method is simple. Someone has a desperate story to tell, and Zweig contrives a way—a chance encounter at a gambling salon at Monte Carlo, a manuscript left among a dead man's belongings—for him or her to tell it. The beauty lies in the act of telling, of exquisite self-exposure, the thrill of sending an illicit message into the unknown. Zweig's contrivances might be deemed obvious, were they not so powerfully effective. *Confusion*, the subtitle of which is *The Private Papers of Privy Councillor R von D*, is a perfect example of his subtle art. These are 'private papers' with a very big difference, for they are scarcely concerned with R von D's life at all. The Privy Councillor has been showered with academic and civic honours, which he mentions casually, almost disdainfully. The true subject of his memoir is a professor of

11

English language and literature in a university in a small town in central Germany. The young Roland, whose name is not revealed until the end of the narrative, enrols as a student in the professor's class. The hitherto lazy and undisciplined youth finds himself enthralled and enchanted by the teacher, whose love and understanding of Shakespeare is fuelled by a deep knowledge of the Elizabethan age—its poetry, its drama, its politics. The professor offers him accommodation in the spare room at the top of the house he shares with his bitter and frustrated wife. It becomes clear, as the delicate and complex story develops, that the professor's passionate and inspirational manner in the lecture hall is a sublimation, as Freud would have noted, for his unsatisfied sexual feelings. Whenever Roland's hero disappears to Berlin, it is with a specific purpose in mind. He goes to notorious bars frequented by male prostitutes and, when he has consumed enough alcohol to give him courage, he approaches and propositions the one he finds most physically attractive. What follows in the morning is best summed up in Shakespeare's Sonnet CXXIX:

Th'expense of spirit in a waste of shame
Is lust in action, and till action, lust
Is perjured, murd'rous, bloody full of blame,
Savage, extreme, rude, cruel, not to trust,
Enjoyed no sooner but despised straight ...

The professor returns to the university after these adventures full of shame and self-loathing, feelings common to male homosexuals in the days when society regarded them as lepers. Zweig recounts in his wonderful memoir *The World of Yesterday*, which was published posthumously, that he was horrified at the sight of the boys, many of them wearing make-up and feminine accessories, lined up along the Kurfürstendamm plying their trade. (A decade later, these boys and their successors would be regarded with something close to affection by W H Auden, Christopher Isherwood and Francis Bacon.) Zweig's 'revulsion' is reflected in the character of the professor, but with a novelist's disinterested compassion. *Confusion* comes to a close with a heartfelt and beautifully resonant coda, in which the dead and forgotten professor is afforded a literary honour by his adoring pupil, a married man with children, more precious than the specious titles bestowed on the privy councillor. "I have never loved anyone more", he writes of the man with whom he once shared a single kiss.

Zweig's stories and novellas could be described as moral fables because they are concerned so potently with the conflict between what ought to be good and what turns out to be bad. In *Letter from an Unknown Woman*, for a long time the most celebrated of these fables thanks to the glorious film Max Ophüls made from it, an unhappy woman writes a letter to the only man she has ever loved. In the story, the man is a callous and self-regarding writer, but in the movie he's a concert pianist, forever on the move. She informs the father of her child, a fact of which he is unaware, that she had to resort to prostitution in order to pay for the boy's education. Prostitutes in English fiction, Moll Flanders and Fanny Hill excepted, tend to be downtrodden, 'fallen' women, but this is *fin-de-siècle* Vienna, where girls of all ages could pursue an alternative career in a thriving market. Zweig sees no reason to moralise because he knows that the correspondent is desperate and it is the nature of her desperation that involves him. He handles with great finesse and literary decorum a story that could easily have been romantic tosh. Ophüls's movie pays homage to a fellow master, for the two men know everything there is to know about the heights and depths of sexual passion. The director's involvement with Zweig's story is demonstrated by the fact that he was able to coax animated performances out of Joan Fontaine and Louis Jourdan, two actors who invariably turned in lifeless, narcissistic performances. The irony here is that the man who pays her to be his mistress is both kinder and more considerate than the novelist with whom she has remained, against all reason, in love.

Twenty-Four Hours in the Life of a Woman, first published in German in 1927, properly merits the over-used description 'haunting'. Zweig is among those rare male writers who see a woman's feelings from a woman's point of view. The old English lady, Mrs C, who confides in an attentive guest at a hotel in Monte Carlo, has been waiting for a decade to cleanse herself of the memory of the twenty-four deluded hours she spent in the company of a handsome Polish gambler. Her husband of twenty-three years had died and she had found herself wandering aimlessly around Europe. Her need to make a confession to a stranger is sparked off by the sudden disappearance from the hotel of the wife of a wealthy businessman. It is rumoured that the woman is in thrall to another younger man. Mrs C bares her soul, and as her story draws to an end she observes: "It has done me good to tell you all this. I feel easier in my mind now and almost light at heart ... thank you for that."

Zweig's trusted formula as a storyteller may sound simple to the point of obviousness, but the artfully constructed framework gives him the freedom to explore his chosen individuals in depth. One soon forgets the artifice as the characters come to vivid life, surprising themselves with their revelations. In *Burning Secret*, which is set in an Austrian spa in the 1920s, a twelve-year-old boy named Edgar, who is there with his mother, is befriended by a baron "from a not particularly illustrious noble family in the Austrian civil service". The Baron is handsome and a determined seducer of attractive women, married or unmarried. The sickly Edgar's mama is already middle-aged, yet she has retained something of her youthful beauty. The Baron uses the gullible and trusting boy as a means of getting closer to the only woman in the hotel who excites him physically. Edgar is overwhelmed by the Baron's attention to him—he has found a friend and companion, not just a father figure. The novella is told in the third person, with the narrative flitting from the child to the mother and thence to the Baron. This is a study in betrayal and jealousy, with the hapless Edgar attaining something like premature manhood. Edgar is granted "a first premonition of the rich variety of life" as a result of his humiliating experience and that, Zweig implies, is a gift to be cherished.

Like all serious novelists, Stefan Zweig was aware of the gulf between the messiness of living and the tidiness of fiction. It was his aim to have the two opposites working in artistic harmony, as he demonstrates in the short story *The Fowler Snared* from the collection *Fantastic Night and Other Stories*. This is a meditation in miniature on the art of storytelling. A writer is on holiday at Cadenabbia on Lake Como. He gets into conversation at the hotel with a man in late middle age, who is, in common with so many of Zweig's characters, cultivated and refined. The man wishes that he was creative himself, rather than a discerning admirer of other men's literary efforts—a discernment that enables him to distinguish between the unexplainable vagaries of life and the questionable orderliness of a certain kind of fiction. He has his own complicated story to tell. On holiday the previous year, at the same hotel, he noticed a couple of German women, probably sisters, in the company of a shy and beautiful sixteen-year-old girl. He supposed she was the daughter of one of them. He took pity on the child, imprisoned as she was by the strait-laced pair, and decided to release her from them by writing her a love letter, unsigned of course, in elegant German, with the odd allusion to Shakespeare. He watched the girl's face as she read his letter. Her smiles and blushes captivated him:

I watched as she sat with idle fingers between the two stitching elders, and I saw how from time to time her hand moved to a particular part of her dress where I was sure the letter was hid. The fascination of the sport grew. That evening I wrote a second letter, and

continued to write to her night after night. It became
more and more engrossing to instil into these letters
the sentiments of a young man in love, to depict the
waxing of an imaginary passion.

But then a real young man appeared, off the
boat from Bellagio, and the girl was convinced
that he was her would-be lover. Longing glances
were exchanged, to the discomposure of the
two older women. All three left the following
morning. The writer listens to this circuitous
account of unrequited love and explains how
he would improve it were he to set it down.
The man is not impressed by his suggested
improvements and leaves him to reflect on truth
and make-believe, both of which are integral
components of this intriguing narrative.

It seems astonishing that these treasures, for
such I consider them to be, were out of print
in Britain and America for over half-a-century.
As late as the 1970s, Zweig was still regarded
as a populist biographer and essayist but not
much more. *Beware of Pity* and the novella *Amok*
were mentioned occasionally, but little else.
The general assumption was that the collapse
of the Austro-Hungarian culture he was born

into in Vienna in 1881, which he describes so rapturously in *The World of Yesterday*, and the horrific carnage of the First World War shrivelled his talent. Reading him on Dickens, Balzac and Dostoevsky—the subjects of the highly successful *Three Masters* (1920; translated in 1930) is a slightly embarrassing experience today, for the essays say more about him than the geniuses he is discussing with respectful enthusiasm. The portrait of Dickens, in particular, does not survive well, because Zweig goes along with the accepted opinion, expressed by G K Chesterton among others, that Dickens was a middle-class, bourgeois humorist with no understanding of the tragic depths into which human beings sink. Dickens's admirer Dostoevsky knew otherwise. The book can be seen as a celebration of a golden age of novel-writing, an age that Zweig had convinced himself had vanished for ever.

It's now clear that Zweig belongs with three very different masters who each perfected the challenging art of the short story and the novella: Maupassant, Turgenev and Chekhov. They let a tale run its natural course, and that's what Zweig does in the works that Pushkin

Press has resurrected in fine new translations by Anthea Bell. The story *Compulsion* in the collection *Wondrak and Other Stories* is perhaps the most personal of them all. Ferdinand, a painter, and his devoted wife Paula have fled Germany for Switzerland, a neutral country in both world wars. They have found a house in an idyllic setting near Lake Zurich. Ferdinand, meanwhile, is living in dread of the postman and what he will bring in his bag. The expected letter (letters and hotels feature prominently in Zweig's fiction) duly arrives in the form of Ferdinand's call-up papers. He decides, against his judgement and his pacifist beliefs, to do as the Fatherland bids him. His rows with Paula become increasingly upsetting. The tension is brilliantly sustained as the reader wonders what Ferdinand will do—renounce the love of his wife for a nationalism he at heart despises. As always in Zweig, the resolution—when it comes—is accidental, the result of the briefest of encounters on a railway platform on the Swiss-German border.

And now comes *Journey into the Past*, which has a distinctly Chekhovian air about it. A young man from a poor background is given employment by a councillor who later entrusts him with the task of opening a branch of his company in Mexico and to bring "ore out of the mountains where it had been slumbering for thousands of years in the mindless sleep of stone" and to build towns and houses and roads with this new-found wealth. The prospect of riches attracts him and in that moment of attraction he and the Councillor's young wife understand that they are madly in love. In the days leading up to his departure they indulge in a frenzy of lovemaking. Years later, the man—now married, with children—returns to Germany. He and the wife of the dead councillor arrange an assignation. Their joint journey into the past surprises them in equal measure, as indeed it does the reader—that anonymous spirit who never failed to command Stefan Zweig's attention and respect, despite the pessimism that finally engulfed him.

PAUL BAILEY 2009

22

JOURNEY INTO
THE PAST

"THERE YOU ARE!" He went to meet her with arms outstretched, almost flung wide. "There you are," he repeated, his voice climbing the scale from surprise to delight ever more clearly, while his tender glance lingered on her beloved form. "I was almost afraid you wouldn't come!"

"Do you really have so little faith in me?" But only her lips playfully uttered this mild reproach, smiling. Her blue eyes lit up, shining with confidence.

"No, not that, I never doubted that—what in this world can be relied on more than your word? But think how foolish I was—suddenly this afternoon, entirely unexpectedly, I can't think why, I felt a spasm of senseless fear. I was afraid something could have happened to you. I wanted to send you a telegram, I wanted to go to you, and just now, when the hands of the

27

clock moved on and still I didn't see you, I was horribly afraid we might miss each other yet again. But thank God, you're here now—"

"Yes, I'm here," she smiled, and once more a star shone brightly from the depths of those blue eyes. "I'm here and I'm ready. Shall we go?"

"Yes, let's go," his lips automatically echoed her. But his motionless body did not move a step, again and again his loving gaze lingered on her incredible presence. Above them, to right and left, the railway tracks of Frankfurt Central Station clanged and clanked with the noise of iron and glass, shrill whistling cut through the tumult in the smoky concourse, twenty boards imperiously displayed different departure and arrival times, complete with the hours and the minutes, while in the maelstrom of the busy crowd he felt that she was the only person really present, removed from time and space in a strange trance of passionate bemusement. In the end she had to remind him, "It's high time we left, Ludwig, we haven't bought tickets yet." Only then did his fixed gaze move away from her, and he took her arm with tender reverence.

The evening express to Heidelberg was unusually full. Disappointed in their expectation that first-class tickets would get them a compartment to themselves, after looking around in vain they finally chose one occupied only by a single grey-haired gentleman leaning back in a corner, half asleep. They were already pleasurably looking forward to an intimate conversation when, shortly before the whistle blew for the train to leave, three more gentlemen strode into the compartment, out of breath and carrying bulging briefcases. The three newcomers were obviously lawyers, in such a state of animation over a trial which had just ended that their lively discussion entirely ruled out the chance of any further conversation, so the couple resigned themselves to sitting opposite one another without saying a word. Only when one of them looked up did he or she see, in the uncertain shade cast like a dark cloud by the lamp, the other's tender glance lovingly looking that way.

With a slight jolt, the train began to move. The rattling of the wheels drowned out the legal conversation, muting it to mere noise. But then, gradually, the jolting and rattling turned to a rhythmic swaying, like a steel cradle rocking

29

the couple into dreams. And while the rattling wheels invisible below them rolled onward, into a future that each of them imagined differently, the thoughts of both returned in reverie to the past.

They had recently met again after an interval of more than nine years. Separated all that time by unimaginable distance, they now felt this first silent intimacy with redoubled force. Dear God, how long and how far apart they had been— nine years and four thousand days had passed between then and this day, this night! How much time, how much lost time, and yet in the space of a second a single thought took him back to the very beginning. What had it been like? He remembered every detail; he had first entered her house as a young man of twenty-three, the curve of his lips covered by the soft down of a young beard. Struggling free early from a childhood of humiliating poverty, growing up as the recipient of free meals provided by charity, he had made his way by giving private tuition, and was embittered before his time by deprivation and the meagre living that was all he earned. Scraping together pennies during his day's work to buy books, studying by night with weary, over-strained nerves, he had completed his studies of chemistry with distinction and, equipped with his professor's special recommendation, he had gone to see the famous industrialist G, distinguished by the honorary title of Privy Councillor and director of the big factory in Frankfurt-am-Main. There he was initially given menial tasks to perform in the laboratory, but soon the Councillor became aware of the serious tenacity of this young man, who immersed himself in his work with all the pent-up force of single-minded determination, and he began taking a particular interest in him. By way of testing his new assistant he gave him increasingly responsible work, and the young man, seeing the possibility of escaping from the dismal prison of poverty, eagerly seized his chance. The more work he was given, the more energetically he tackled it, so that in a very short time he rose from being one of dozens of assistants to becoming his employer's right-hand man, trusted to conduct secret experiments, his "young friend", as the Councillor benevolently liked to call him. For although the young man did not know it, a probing mind inside the private door of the director's office was assessing his suitability for higher things, and

31

while the ambitious assistant thought he was merely mastering his daily work in a mood of furious energy, his almost invisible employer had him marked out for a great future. For some years now the ageing Councillor, who was often kept at home and sometimes even in bed by his very painful sciatica, had been looking for a totally reliable and intellectually well-qualified private secretary, a man to whom he could turn for discussion of the firm's most confidential patents, as well as those experiments that had to be made with all the requisite discretion. And at last he seemed to have found him. One day he put an unexpected proposition to the startled young man: how would he like to give up the furnished room he rented in the suburbs, and take up residence in Councillor G's spacious villa, where he would be closer to hand for his employer? The young man was surprised by this proposition, coming as it did out of the blue, but the Councillor was even more surprised when, after a day spent thinking it over, the young man firmly declined the honour of his employer's offer, rather clumsily hiding his outright refusal behind thin excuses. Eminent scientist as the Councillor was in his own field, he did not have enough psychological experience to guess the true reason for this refusal, and the defiant young man may not even have acknowledged it to himself. It was, in fact, a kind of perverted pride, the painful sense of shame left by a childhood spent in dire poverty. Coming to adulthood as a private tutor in the distastefully ostentatious houses of the *nouveaux riches*, feeling that he was a nameless hybrid being somewhere between a servant and a companion, part and yet not part of the household, an ornamental item like the magnolias on the table, placed there and then cleared away again as required, he found himself brimming over with hatred for his employers and the sphere in which they lived, the heavy, ponderous furniture, the lavishly decorated rooms, the over-rich meals, all the wealth that he shared only on sufferance. He had gone through much in those houses: the hurtful remarks of impertinent children; the even more hurtful pity of the lady of the house when she handed him a few banknotes at the end of the month; the ironic, mocking looks of the maids, who were always ready to be cruel to the upper servants, when he moved into a new house with his plain wooden trunk and had to hang his only suit and put away his grey, darned underwear, that infallible sign of poverty, in a wardrobe that was not his own. No, never again, he had sworn to himself, he would never live in a strange house again, never go back to riches until they belonged to him, never again let his neediness show, or allow presents tactlessly given to hurt his feelings. Never, never again. Outwardly his title of *Doctor*, cheap but impenetrable armour, made up for his low social status, and at the office his fine achievements disguised the still sore and festering wounds of his youth, when he had felt ashamed of his poverty and of taking charity. So no, he was not going to sell the handful of freedom he now had, his jealously guarded privacy, not for any sum of money. And he declined the flattering invitation, even at the risk of wrecking his career, with excuses and evasions.

Soon, however, unforeseen circumstances left him no choice. The Councillor's state of health deteriorated so much that he had to spend a long time bedridden, and could not even keep in touch with his office by telephone. The presence of a private secretary now became an urgent necessity and finally, if the young man did not want to lose his job, he could no longer resist his employer's repeated and pressing requests. God knows, he thought, the move to the villa had been difficult for him; he still clearly remembered the day when he first rang the bell of the grand house, which was rather in the old Franconian style, in the Bockenheimer Landstrasse The evening before, so that his poverty would not be too obvious, he had hastily bought new underwear, a reasonably good black suit and new shoes, spending his savings on them—and those savings were meagre, for on his salary, which was not high, he was also keeping an old mother and two sisters in a remote provincial town. And this time a hired man delivered the ugly trunk containing his earthly goods ahead of him—the trunk that he hated because of all the memories it brought back. All the same, discomfort rose like some thick obstruction in his throat when a white-gloved servant formally opened the door to him, and even in the front hall he met with the satiated, self-satisfied atmosphere of wealth. Deep-piled carpets that softly swallowed up his footsteps were waiting, tapestries hung on the walls even in the hall, demanding solemn study, there were carved wooden doors with heavy bronze handles, clearly not intended to be touched by a visitor's own hand but opened by a respectfully bowing servant. In his defiantly bitter mood, he found all this oppressive. It was both heady and unwelcome. And when the servant showed him into the guest-room with its three windows, the place intended as his permanent residence, his sense of being an intruder who was out of place here gained the upper hand. Yesterday he had been living in a draughty little fourth-floor back room, with a wooden bedstead and a tin basin to wash in, and now he was supposed to make himself at home here, where every item of the furnishings seemed boldly opulent, aware of its monetary value, and looked back at him with scorn as a man who was merely tolerated here. All he had brought with him, even he himself in his own clothes, shrank to miserable proportions in this spacious, well-lit room. His one coat, ridiculously occupying the big, wide wardrobe, looked like a hanged man; his few washing things and his shabby shaving kit lay on the roomy, marble-tiled wash-stand like something he had coughed up or a tool carelessly left there by a workman; and instinctively he threw a shawl over the hard, ugly wooden trunk, envying it for its ability to lie in hiding here, while he himself stood inside these four walls like a burglar caught in the act. In vain he tried to counter his ashamed, angry sense of being nothing by reminding himself that he had been specifically asked for, pressingly invited to come. But the comfortable solidity of the items around him kept demolishing his arguments. He felt small again, insignificant, of no account in the face of this ostentatious, magnificent world of money, servants, flunkeys and other hangers-on, human furniture that had been bought and could be lent out. It was as if his own nature had been stolen from him. And now, when the servant tapped lightly at the door and appeared, his face frozen and his bearing stiff, to announce that the lady of the house had sent to ask if the doctor would call on her, he felt, as he hesitantly followed the man through the suite of rooms, that for the first time in years his stature was shrinking, his shoulders already stooping into an obsequious bow, and after a gap of years the uncertainty and confusion he had known as a boy revived in him.

However, no sooner had he approached her for the first time than he felt an agreeable sensation as his inner tension relaxed, and even before, as he straightened his back after bowing to her, his eyes took in the face and figure of the woman speaking to him, her words had come irresistibly to his ears. Those first words were "Thank you", spoken in so frank and natural a tone that they dispersed the dark clouds of ill humour hanging over him and went to his heart as he heard them. "Thank you very much, doctor," she said, cordially offering him her hand, "for accepting my husband's invitation in the end. I hope I shall soon be able to show you how extremely grateful to you I myself am. It may not have been easy for you; a man doesn't readily give up his freedom, but perhaps it will reassure you to know that you have placed two people deeply in your debt. For my part, I will do all I can to make you feel that this house is your home."

Something inside him pricked up its ears. How did she know that he had been unwilling to give up his freedom, how was it that her first words went straight to the festering, scarred, sensitive part of his nature, straight to the seat of his nervous terror of losing his independence to become only a hired servant, living here on sufferance? How had she managed to brush all such thoughts of his aside with that first gesture of her hand? Instinctively he looked up at her, and only now was he aware of a warm, sympathetic glance confidently waiting for him to return it.

There was something serenely gentle, re-assuring, cheerfully confident about that face. Her pure brow, still youthfully smooth, radiated clarity, and above it the demurely matronly style in which she parted her hair seemed almost too old for her. Her hair itself was a dark mass falling in deep waves, while the dress around her shapely shoulders and coming up to her throat was also dark, making the calm light in her face seem all the brighter. She resembled a bourgeois Madonna, a little like a nun in her high-necked dress, and there was a maternal kindness in all her movements. Now she gracefully came a step closer, her smile anticipating the thanks on his own faltering lips. "Just one request, my first, and at our first meeting, too. I know that when people who haven't been acquainted for very long are living in the same house, that's always a problem, and there's only one way of dealing with it—honesty. So please, if you feel ill at ease here in any way, if any kind of situation or arrangement troubles you, do tell me about it freely. You are my husband's private secretary, I am his wife, we are linked by that double duty, so please let us be honest with one another."

He took her hand, and the pact was sealed. From that first moment he felt at home in the house. The magnificence of the rooms was no longer a hostile threat to him, indeed on the contrary, he immediately saw it as the essential setting for the elegant distinction that, in this house, muted and made harmonious all that seemed inimical, confused and contradictory outside it. But only gradually did he come to realize how exquisite artistic taste made mere financial value subject to a higher order here, and how that muted rhythm of existence was instinctively becoming part of his own life and his own conversation. He felt curiously reassured— all keen, vehement, passionate emotions became devoid of malice and edginess. It was as if the deep carpets, the tapestries on the walls, the coloured shutters absorbed the brightness and noise of the street, and at the same time he felt that this sense of order did not arise spontaneously, but derived from the presence of the quietly spoken woman whose smile was always so kindly. And the following weeks and months made him pleasantly aware of what he had felt, as if by magic, in those first minutes. With a fine sense of tact, she gradually and without making him feel any compulsion drew him into the inner life of this house. Sheltered but not guarded, he sensed attentive sympathy bent on him as if at a distance; any little wishes of his were granted almost as soon as he had expressed them, and granted so discreetly, as if by household elves, that they made explicit thanks impossible. When he had been leafing through a portfolio of valuable engravings one evening and particularly admired one of them—it happened to be Rembrandt's *Faust*—he found a framed reproduction hanging over his desk two days later. If he mentioned that a friend had recommended a certain book, there would be a copy on his bookshelves next day. His room was adapting, as if unconsciously, to his wishes and habits; often he did not notice exactly what details had changed at first, but just felt that the place was more comfortable,

41

warmer, brighter, until he realized, say, that the embroidered Oriental coverlet he had admired in a shop window was covering the ottoman, or the light now shone through a raspberry-coloured silk shade. He liked the atmosphere here better and better for its own sake, and was quite unwilling to leave the house, where he had also become a close friend of a boy of eleven, and greatly enjoyed accompanying him and his mother to the theatre or to concerts. Without his realizing it, all that he did outside his working hours was bathed in the mild moonlight of her calm presence.

From that first meeting he had loved this woman, but passionately as his feelings surged over him, following him even into his dreams, the crucial factor that would shake him to the core was still lacking—his conscious realization that what, denying his true feelings, he still called admiration, respect and devotion was in fact love—a burning, unbounded, absolute and passionate love. Some kind of servile instinct in him forcibly suppressed that realization; she seemed so distant, too far away, too high above him, a radiant woman surrounded by a circle of stars, armoured by her wealth and by all that

42

he had ever known of women before. It would have seemed blasphemous to think of her as a sexual being, subject to the same laws of the blood as the few other women who had come his way during his youth spent in servitude: the maidservant at the manor house who, just once, had opened her bedroom door to the tutor, curious to see if a man who had studied at university did it the same way as the coachman and the farm labourer; the seamstress he had met in the dim light of the street lamps on his way home. No, this was different. She shone down from another sphere, beyond desire, pure and inviolable, and even in his most passionate dreams he did not venture so far as to undress her. In boyish confusion, he loved the fragrance of her presence, appreciating all her movements as if they were music, glad of her confidence in him and always fearing to show her any of the overwhelming emotion that stirred within him, an emotion still without a name, but long since fully formed and glowing in its place of concealment.

But love truly becomes love only when, no longer an embryo developing painfully in the darkness of the body, it ventures to confess

43

itself with lips and breath. However hard it tries to remain a chrysalis, a time comes when the intricate tissue of the cocoon tears, and out it falls, dropping from the heights to the farthest depths, falling with redoubled force into the startled heart. That happened quite late, in the second year of his life as one of the household.

One Sunday the Councillor had asked him to come into his study, and the fact that, unusually for him, he closed the door behind them after a quick greeting, then calling through on the house telephone to say they were not to be disturbed, in itself strongly suggested that something special was about to be communicated. The old man offered him a cigar and lit it with ceremony, as if to gain time before launching into a speech that he had obviously thought out carefully in advance. He began by thanking his assistant at length for his services. In every way, said the Councillor, he had even exceeded his own confident expectations and borne out his personal liking for him; he, the Councillor, had never had cause to regret entrusting even his most intimate business affairs to a man he had known for so short a time. Well, he went on, yesterday important news from overseas had reached the company, and he did not hesitate to tell his assistant at once—the new chemical process, with which he was familiar, called for considerable amounts of certain ores, and the Councillor had just been informed by telegram that large deposits of the metals concerned had been found in Mexico. Swift action was vital if they were to be acquired for the company, and their mining and exploitation must be organized on the spot before any American companies seized this great opportunity. That in turn called for a reliable but young and energetic man. To him personally, said the Councillor, it was a painful blow to deprive himself of his trusted and reliable assistant, but when the board of directors met he had thought it his duty to suggest him as the best and indeed the only suitable man for the job. He would feel himself compensated by knowing that he could guarantee him a brilliant future. In the two years it would take to set up the business in Mexico, the young man could not only build up a small fortune for himself, thanks to the large remuneration he would receive, he could also look forward to holding a senior position in the company on his return. "Indeed," concluded the Councillor, spreading his hands in a congratulatory gesture, "I feel as if I saw you sitting here in my place some day, carrying through to its end the work on which, old as I now am, I embarked three decades ago."

Such a proposition, coming suddenly out of a clear sky—how could it not go to an ambitious man's head? There at last was the door, flung wide as if by the blast of an explosion, showing him the way out of the prison of poverty, the lightless world of service and obedience, away from the constantly obsequious attitude of a man forced to act and think with humility. He gazed avidly at the papers and telegrams before him, seeing hieroglyphics gradually formed into the imposing if still vague contours of this mighty plan. Numbers suddenly came cascading down on him, thousands, hundreds of thousands, millions to be managed, accounted for, acquired, the fiery atmosphere of commanding power in which, dazed and with his heart beating fast, he suddenly rose from his dull, subservient sphere of life as if in a dreamlike balloon. And over and above all this, it was not just money on offer, not just business deals and ventures, a game played for high stakes, responsibility—no, something much more alluring tempted him. Here was the chance to fashion events, to be a pioneer. A great task lay ahead, the creative occupation of bringing ore out of the mountains where it had been slumbering for thousands of years in the mindless sleep of stone, of driving galleries into that stone, building towns, seeing houses rise up, roads spread out, putting mechanical diggers to work, and cranes circling in the air. Behind the mere framework of calculations a wealth of fantastic yet vivid images began to form—farmsteads, farmhouses, factories, warehouses, a new part of the world of men where as yet there was nothing, and it would be for him to set it up, directing and regulating operations. Sea air, spiced by the intoxication of all that is far distant, suddenly entered the small, comfortably upholstered study; figures stacked up into a fantastic sum. And in an ever more heated frenzy of exhilaration that gave wings to every decision, he had it all summarized in broad outline, and the purely practical details were agreed. A cheque for a

47

sum he could never have expected was suddenly crackling crisply in his hand, and after the agreement had been reiterated, it was decided that he would leave on the next Southern Line steamer in ten days' time. Then he had left the Councillor's study, still heated by the swirl of figures, reeling at the idea of the possibilities that had been conjured up, and once outside the door he stood staring wildly around him for a moment, wondering if the entire conversation could have been a phantasmagoria conjured up by wishful thinking. The space of a wing-beat had raised him from the depths into the sparkling sphere of fulfilment; his blood was still in such turmoil after so stormy an ascent that he had to shut his eyes for a moment. He closed them as one might take a deep breath, simply to be in control again, sensing his inner being more powerfully and as if separated from himself. This state of mind lasted for a minute, but then, as he looked up again refreshed, and his eyes wandered around the familiar room outside the study, they fell as if by chance on a picture hanging over the large chest, and lingered there. It was her portrait. Her picture looked back at him with lips gently closed, curving in a calm smile that also seemed to have a deeper meaning, as if it had understood every word of what was going on inside him. And then, in that second, an idea that he had entirely overlooked until now flashed through his mind—if he took up the position offered to him, it meant leaving this house. My God, he said to himself, leaving *her*. Like a knife, the thought cut through the proudly swelling sail of his delight. And in that one second of uncontrolled surprise the whole artificially piled edifice of his imaginings collapsed, crushing his heart, and with a sudden painful jolt of the heart muscle he felt how painful, how almost deadly the idea of doing without her was to him. Leaving her, oh God, leaving her—how could he ever have contemplated it, how could he have made that decision as if he still belonged to himself, as if he were not held here, in her presence, by all the bonds of his emotions, their deepest roots? The idea broke out violently, it was elemental, a quivering physical pain, a blow struck through his whole body from the top of his skull to the bottom of his heart, a lightning bolt tearing across the night sky and illuminating everything. And now, in that blinding light, it was impossible not to realize that every nerve and fibre of his being was flowering with love for her, his dear one. No sooner had he silently uttered the magical word *love* than countless little associations and memories shot sparkling through his mind, with the extraordinary speed that only the utmost alarm can conjure up. Every one of them cast bright light on his feelings, on all the little details that he had never before ventured to admit to himself or understand. And only at this point did he realize how utterly he had been in thrall to her, and for how long—many months now.

Hadn't it been during Easter week this year, when she went to stay with her family for three days, that he had paced restlessly from room to room as if lost, unable to read a book, his mind in turmoil, although he could not say why? And on the night when she was to return, hadn't he stayed up until one in the morning to hear her footsteps? Hadn't his nervous impatience kept sending him downstairs too soon, to see if the car wasn't coming yet? He remembered how, when his hand accidentally brushed hers at the theatre, a frisson ran from the touch of their fingers to the back of his neck. Now a hundred such little flashes of memory, trifles of which he had hardly been aware, raced stormily into his mind, into his blood, as if every dam had been breached, and they all made straight for his heart and came together there. Instinctively, he pressed his hand to his chest, where that heart was beating so violently, and now there was no help for it, he could no longer keep from admitting what his diffident and respectful instinct had so carefully managed to obscure for so long—he could not live now away from her presence. To be without that mild light shining on his way for two years, two months, even just two weeks, to enjoy no more of their pleasant conversations in the evenings—no, it was impossible to bear such a thought. And what had filled him with pride only ten minutes earlier, the mission to Mexico, the thought of his rise to have command of creative power, had shrunk within a second, had burst like a sparkling soap bubble. All that it meant now was distance, absence, a dungeon, banishment and exile, annihilation, a deprivation that he could not survive. No, it was impossible—his hand was already moving to the door handle again, he was on the point of going back into the study to tell the Councillor that he wouldn't do it, to say he felt unworthy of the mission, he would rather stay here. But anxiety spoke up, warning him: not now! He must not prematurely betray a secret that was only just revealing itself to him. And he wearily withdrew his fevered hand from the cool metal.

Once again he looked at her picture—the glance of her eyes seemed to be gazing ever deeper into him, but he could not see the smile around her mouth any more. Instead, he thought, she looked gravely, almost sadly out of the picture, as if to say, "You wanted to forget me." He couldn't bear that painted yet living gaze. He stumbled to his room, sinking on the bed with a strange sensation of horror almost like fainting, but curiously pervaded by a mysterious sweetness. Feverishly, he thought back to all that had happened to him in this house since he first arrived, and everything, even the most insignificant detail, now had a different meaning and appeared in a different light; it was all irradiated by the inner light of understanding, its weight was light as it soared up in the heated air of passion. He remembered all the kindness she had shown him. He was still surrounded by it; his eyes looked for the signs of it, he felt the things that her hand had touched, and they all had something of the joy of her presence in them. She was there in those inanimate objects; he sensed her friendly thoughts in them. And that certainty of her goodwill to him overwhelmed him with passion, yet deep below its current something in his nature still resisted, like a stone—there was something left unthought, something not yet cleared out of the way, and it had to be cleared out of the way before his emotions could flow freely. Very cautiously, he made his way towards that dark place in the depths of his emotion, he knew already what it meant, yet he dared not touch it. But the current kept driving him back to that one place, that one question. And it was this: was there not—he dared not say love, but at least liking for him on her part, shown in all those small attentive acts, a mild affection, if without passion, in the way she listened for his presence and showed concern for him? That sombre question went through him, heavy, black waves rose in his blood, breaking again and again, but they could not roll it away. If only I could think clearly, he said to himself, but his thoughts were in too much passionate turmoil, mingling with confused dreams and wishes, and pain was churned up again and again from the uttermost depths of his being. So he lay there on his bed for perhaps an hour or two hours, entirely outside himself, sensations dulled by his numbing mixture of emotions, until suddenly a gentle tapping at his door brought him back to himself. The cautious tapping of slender knuckles; he thought he recognized their touch. He jumped up and ran to the door.

There she stood before him, smiling. "Oh, doctor, why don't you come down? The bell has rung for dinner twice."

She spoke almost in high spirits, as if she took a little pleasure in catching him out in a small act of negligence. But as soon as she saw his face, with his hair clinging around it in damp strands, his dazed eyes shyly avoiding hers, she herself turned pale.

"For God's sake, what has happened to you?" she faltered, and the tone of horror in her breaking voice went through him like desire. "Nothing, nothing," he said, quickly pulling himself together. "I was deep in thought, that's all. The whole thing was too much for me, too sudden."

"What? What whole thing? Tell me!"

"Don't you know? Didn't the Councillor tell you anything about it?"

"No, nothing!" she urged him impatiently, almost driven mad by the nervous, burning, evasive expression in his eyes. "What's happened? Tell me, please tell me!"

Then he summoned up all the strength in him to look at her clearly and without blushing. "The Councillor has been kind enough to give me an important and responsible mission, and I have accepted it. In ten days' time I'm sailing for Mexico, to stay there for two years."

"Two years! Dear God!" It was a cry rather than words, as her own horror shot up from deep within her. And she put out her hands in instinctive denial. It was useless for her to try, next moment, denying the feeling that had burst out of her, for already (and just how had that happened?) he had taken the hands she so passionately reached out to fend off her fear in his own, and before they knew it their trembling bodies were both aflame. Countless hours and days of unconscious longing and thirst were quenched in an endless kiss.

He had not drawn her to him, she had not drawn him to her. they had met as if driven together by a storm, falling clasped together into a bottomless abyss of the unconscious, and sinking into it was like a sweet yet burning trance—emotions too long pent up poured out in a single second, inflamed by the magnetism of chance. Only slowly, as the lips that had clung together parted, as they were still shaken by the unreality of it all, did he look into her eyes and saw a strange light behind their tender darkness. And only then was he overwhelmed by the realization that this woman, the woman he loved, must have loved him in return for a long time, for weeks, months, years, keeping tenderly silent, glowing with maternal feeling, until a moment such as this struck through her soul. The incredible nature of the realization was intoxicating. To think that he was loved, loved by the woman he had thought beyond his reach—heaven opened up, endless and flooded with light. This was the radiant noon of his life. But at the same time it all collapsed next moment, splintering sharply. For the realization that she loved him was also a farewell.

The two of them spent the ten days until his departure in a constant state of wild, ecstatic frenzy. The sudden explosive force of the feelings they had now confessed had broken down all dams and barriers, all morality and pride. They fell on one another like animals, hot and greedy, whenever they met to snatch two stolen minutes in a dark corridor, behind a door, in a corner. Hand made its way to hand, lips to lips, the restless blood of one met its kindred blood in the other, each longed feverishly for the other, every nerve burned for the sensuous touch of foot, hand, dress, some living part of the yearning body. At the same time they had to exert self-control in the house, she to hide the love that kept blazing up in her from her husband, her son, the servants, he to remain intellectually capable of the calculations, meetings and deliberations for which he was now responsible. They could never snatch more than seconds, quivering, furtive seconds when danger lay in wait, they could fleetingly approach each other only with their hands, their lips, their eyes, a greedily stolen kiss, and each, already intoxicated, was further intoxicated by the other's hazy, sultry, smouldering presence. But it was never enough, they both felt that, never enough. So they wrote each other burning love letters, slipping ardent notes into one another's hands like school-children. He found hers in the evening, under the pillow on which he could get no sleep; she in turn found his in her coat pockets, and all these notes ended in a desperate cry asking the unhappy question: how could they bear it, a sea, a world, uncounted months, uncounted weeks, two years between blood and blood, glance and glance? They thought of nothing else, they dreamed of nothing else, and neither of them had an answer to the question, only their hands, eyes and lips, the unconscious servants of their passion, moved back and forth, longing to come together, pledging inner constancy. And then those stolen moments of touching, embracing fervently behind doors drawn nearly closed, those fearful moments would overflow with lust and fear at once, in Bacchanalian frenzy.

However, although he longed for it he was never granted full possession of the beloved body that he sensed, through her unfeeling, obstructive dress, passionately moving, feeling it pressing as if hot and naked against his—he never came really close to her in that too brightly lit house, always awake and full of ears to hear them. Only on the last day, when she came to his room, already cleared, on the pretext of helping him to pack but really to say a last goodbye, and stumbled and fell against the ottoman as she swayed under the onslaught of his embrace— then, when his kisses were already burning on the curve of her breasts under the dress he had pulled up, and were greedily travelling over the hot, white skin to the place where her heart beat in response to his own as she gasped for breath, when in that moment of surrender the gift of her body was almost his, then in her passion she stammered out a last plea. "Not now! Not here! I beg you!"

And even his heated blood was still so obedient, so much in thrall to her, so respectful of the woman he had loved as a sacred being for so long, that once again he controlled his ardour and moved away as she rose, swaying, and hid her face from him. He himself turned away too and stood there, trembling and fighting with his instincts, so visibly affected by the grief of his disappointment that she knew how much his love, denied fulfilment, was suffering because of her. Then, back in command of her own feelings again, she came close and quietly comforted him. "I couldn't do it here, in my own house, in his own house. But when you come back, yes, whenever you like."

The train stopped with a clatter, screeching in the vice-like hold of the brake applied to it. Like a dog waking under the touch of the whip, his eyes woke from reverie, and—what a happy moment of recognition—look, there she was, his beloved who had been so far away for so long. Now she sat there, close enough for him to feel her breathing. The brim of her hat cast a little shadow on her face as she leaned back. But as if, unconsciously, she had understood that he wanted to see her face she sat up straight, and looked at him with a mild smile. "Darmstadt," she said, glancing out of the window. "One more station to go." He did not reply. He just sat looking at her. Time is helpless, he thought to himself, helpless in the face of our feelings. Nine years have passed, and not a note in her voice is different, not a nerve in my body hears her in any other way. Nothing is lost, nothing is past and over, her presence is as much of a tender delight now as it was then.

He looked with passion at her quietly smiling mouth, which he could hardly remember kissing in the past, and then down at the white hands lying relaxed and at rest on her lap; he longed to bend and touch them with his lips, or take those quietly folded hands in his, just for a second, one second! But the talkative gentlemen sharing the compartment were already beginning to look at him curiously, and for the sake of his secret he leaned back again in silence. Once more they sat opposite one another without a sign or a word, and only their eyes met and kissed.

Outside a whistle blew, the train began to roll out of the station once more, and the swinging, swaying monotony of that steel cradle rocked him back into his memories. Ah, the dark, endless years between then and now, a grey sea between shore and shore, between heart and heart! What had it been like? There was a memory that he did not want to touch, he did not wish to recollect the moment of their last goodbye, the moment on the station platform in the city where, today, he had been waiting for her with his heart wide open. No, away with it, it was over and not to be thought of any more, it was too terrible. His thoughts flew back, back again; another landscape, another time opened up in his dreams, conjured up by the rapid rhythm of the rattling wheels. He had gone to Mexico with a heart torn in two, and he managed to endure the first months there, the first terrible weeks that passed before any message from her arrived, only by cramming his head full of figures and drafted designs, by exhausting himself physically with long rides and expeditions out into the country, and what seemed endless negotiations and enquiries, but he carried them through with determination. From morning to night, he locked himself into the engine-house of the company, constantly at work hammering out numbers, talking, writing all the time, only to hear his inner voice desperately crying out one name, hers. He numbed himself with work as another man might with alcohol or drugs, merely to deaden the strength of his emotions. But every evening, however tired he was, he sat down to describe on sheet after sheet of paper, writing for hour after hour, everything that he had done in the day, and by every post he sent whole bundles of these feverishly written pages to a cover address on which they had agreed, so that his distant beloved could follow his life hourly as she used to at home, and he felt her mild gaze resting on his daily work, sharing it in her mind over a thousand sea miles, over hills and horizons. The letters he received from her were his reward. Her handwriting was upright, her words calm, betraying passion but in disciplined form. They told him first, without complaint, about her daily life, and it was as if he felt her steady blue gaze bent on him, although without her smile, the faint, reassuring smile which removed all that was severe from any gravity. These letters had been food and drink to the lonely man. In his own passionate emotion, he took them with him on journeys through the plains and the mountains, he had pockets specially sewn to his saddle to protect them from sudden cloudbursts and the rivers that they had to ford on surveying expeditions. He had read those letters so often that he knew them by heart, word for word, he had unfolded them so often that the creases in the paper were wearing transparent, and certain words were blurred by kisses and tears. Sometimes, when he was alone and knew that no one was near him, he began reading them aloud in her own tone of voice, magically conjuring up the presence of his distant love. Sometimes he suddenly rose in the night when he had thought of a particular word, a sentence, a closing salutation, put on the light to find it again and to dream of the image of her hand in the written characters, moving on up from that hand to her arm, her shoulder, her head, her whole physical presence transported over land and sea. And like a man chopping trees down in the jungle, he chopped into the wild and still impenetrably menacing time ahead of him with berserk strength and frenzy, impatient to see it thinning out, to have his return in sight, his journey home, the prospect that he had imagined a thousand times of the moment when they would first embrace again. He had hung a calendar over the bed roughly knocked together for him in his quickly constructed wooden house with its corrugated iron roof in the new workers' colony, and every evening he would cross off the day he had just worked his way through—though he often impatiently crossed it off as early as midday—and he counted and re-counted the ever-diminishing black and red series of days still to be endured: four hundred and twenty, four hundred and nineteen, four hundred and eighteen days to go before they met again. For he was not counting, as other people have done since the birth of Christ, from a beginning but only up to a certain time, the time of his return. And whenever that span of time reached a round number, four hundred or three hundred and fifty or three hundred, or when it was her birthday or name-day, the day when he first saw her or the day when she first revealed her own feelings for him—on such days he always gave a kind of party for those around him, who wondered why, and in their ignorance asked questions. He gave money to the *mestizos*' dirty children and brandy to the workers, who shouted and capered around like wild brown foals, he put on his own Sunday best and had wine brought, and the finest of the canned food. A flag flew, a flame of joy, from a specially erected flagpole, and if neighbours or his assistants, feeling curious, asked what saint's day or other strange occasion he was celebrating, he only smiled and said, "Never mind that, just celebrate it with me!"

So it went on for weeks and months, a year worked its way to death and then another half a year, then there were only seven small, wretched, poor little weeks left until the day appointed for his return. In his boundless impatience he had long ago worked out how long the voyage would take, and to the astonishment of the clerks in the shipping office had booked and paid for his passage on the *Arkansas* a hundred days before she was due to leave.

Then came the disastrous day that pitilessly tore up not only his calendar but, with total indifference, the lives and thoughts of millions, leaving them in shreds. A day of disaster indeed—early in the morning, in his capacity as a surveyor, he had ridden across the sulphur-yellow plain and up into the mountains with horses and mules, taking two foremen and a party of labourers, to investigate a new drilling site where it was thought there might be magnesite. The *mestizos* hammered, dug, pounded and generally investigated the site under a pitiless sun that blazed down from overhead, and was reflected back again at a right angle from the bare rock. But like a man possessed he drove the workers on, would not allow his thirsty tongue the hundred paces it would take him to go to the quickly dug trench for water—he wanted to get back to the post office and see her letter, her words. And when they had not reached the full depth of the site on the third day, and the trial borehole was still being drilled, he was overcome by a senseless longing for her message, a thirst for her words, which deranged him so far that he decided to ride back alone all night, just to collect the letter that must surely have come in the post yesterday. He simply left the others in their tent and, accompanied only by one servant, rode along a dangerously dark bridle path all night to the railway station. But when in the morning, freezing from the icy cold of the mountain range, they finally rode their steaming horses into the little town, an unusual sight met their eyes. The few white settlers had left their work and were standing around the station in the midst of a shouting, questioning, stupidly gaping throng of *mestizos* and native Indians. It was difficult to make a way through this agitated crowd, but once they had reached the post office they found unexpected news waiting. Telegrams had come from the coast— Europe was at war, Germany against France, Austria against Russia. He refused to believe it, dug his spurs into the flanks of his stumbling horse so hard that the frightened animal reared, whinnying, and raced away to the government building, where he heard even more shattering news. It was all true, and even worse, Britain had also declared war. The seven seas were closed to Germans. An iron curtain had come down between the two continents, cutting them off from each other for an incalculable length of time.

It was useless for him to pound the table with his clenched fist in his first fury, as if to strike out at an invisible foe; millions of helpless people were now raging in the same way as the dungeon walls of their destiny closed in on them. He immediately weighed up all the possibilities of smuggling himself across to Europe by some bold and cunning means, thus checkmating Fate, but the British consul, a friend of his who happened to be present, indicated with a cautious note of warning in his voice that he personally was obliged to keep an eye on all his movements from now on. So he could comfort himself only with the hope, soon to be disappointed, as it was for millions of others, that such madness could not last long, and within a few weeks or a few months this foolish prank played by diplomats and generals left to their own devices would be over. Before long, something else was added to that thin fibre of hope, a stronger power and better able to numb his feelings—work. In cables sent by way of Sweden, his company commissioned him to prevent possible sequestration by registering his Mexican branch of it independently and running it, with a few figureheads appointed to the board, as a Mexican firm. This task called for the utmost managerial energy. Since the war itself, that imperious entrepreneur, also wanted ore from the mines, production must be speeded up and the company's work was redoubled. It required all his powers, and drowned out even the echo of any thoughts of his own. He worked with fanatical intensity for twelve or fourteen hours a day, sinking into bed in the evening worn down by the crushing weight of numbers, to sleep dreamlessly,

Yet all the same, while he thought his feelings were unchanged, his passionate inner tension gradually relaxed. It is not in human nature to live entirely on memories, and just as the plants and every living structure need nourishment from the soil and new light from the sky, if their colours are not to fade and their petals to drop, even such apparently unearthly things as dreams need a certain amount of nourishment from the senses, some tender pictorial aid, or their blood will run thin and their radiance be dimmed. And so it was with this passionate man before he even noticed it. When weeks, months, and finally a year and then a second year brought not a single message from her, not a written word, no sign, her picture gradually began to fade. Every day consumed in work made another grain or so of ash settle over her memory; it still showed through, like the red glow under the ashes in the grate, but finally the grey layer grew thicker and thicker. He still sometimes took out her letters, but the ink had faded, the words no longer went straight to his heart, and once he was shocked, looking at her photograph, to find that he could no longer remember the colour of her eyes. And it was less and less often that he picked up those once precious proofs of love, the letters that had magically given him new life, without realizing that he was tired of her eternal silence, tired of talking senselessly to a shadow that never

70

answered. In addition the mining business, which was soon doing very well, threw him together with other people, other partners; he sought out company, friends, women. And when a trip in the third year of the war took him to the house of a prosperous German businessman in Vera Cruz, and he met the man's daughter, a quiet, blonde, home-loving girl, fear of being always alone in the middle of a world rushing headlong into hatred, war and madness overcame him. He quickly made up his mind and proposed marriage. Then came a child, a second followed, living flowers flourishing on the forgotten grave of his love. Now the circle was closed; all was busy activity outside it, inside there was domestic calm, and after four or five years he would not have known the man he once was.

But then there came a day full of stormy emotions and the sound of bells, when the telegraph wires hummed, and loud voices were raised all the streets, proclaiming in large letters the news that peace had finally been made, when the British and Americans in town celebrated the destruction of his native land with loud and inconsiderate rejoicing. On that day, revived by memories of his country, which he loved again in its time of misfortune, her figure too came back into his mind, forcing its way into his emotions. How had she lived through those years of misery and deprivation on which the newspapers here dwelt at length, and with relish, with much busy activity on the part of journalists? Had her house, his house, been spared the upheavals and looting, were her husband and her son still alive? In the middle of the night he rose from the side of his peacefully sleeping wife, put on a light, and spent five hours until dawn writing a letter that seemed as if it would never end, a letter in which he told her, soliloquizing to himself, all about his life in the last five years. After two months, when he had almost forgotten writing his own letter, the answer came—undecidedly, he weighed the large envelope in his hands. Even the familiar handwriting suggested sub-version. He dared not break the seal at once, as if, like Pandora's box, this sealed letter contained something forbidden. He carried it around with him for two days in his breast pocket, and sometimes he felt his heart beating against it. But the letter, once it was opened at last, was neither obtrusively over-familiar nor cold and formal. Its calm handwriting conveyed the tender affection that he had always liked so much in her. Her husband had died at the very beginning of the war, she wrote; she hardly liked to mourn him too much, for it meant that he had been spared a great deal. He did not live to see the danger to his company, the occupation of their city, the misery of his own nation, which had become drunk on the idea of victory far too soon. She herself and her son were in good health, and she was so glad to hear good news of him, better than she could give of herself. She congratulated him on his marriage in honest and unequivocal terms; instinctively he assessed them warily, but no concealed undertone marred their clear meaning. It was all said frankly, without any ostentatious sentimental pathos, all the past seemed to be resolved in the purity of her continued sympathy, passion was transfigured as bright, crystalline friendship. He had never expected any less of her distinction of mind, yet sensing her clear, sure nature (he thought he was suddenly looking into her eyes again, grave and yet smiling in reflected kindness), sensing all that, a kind of grateful emotion overcame him. He sat down at once and wrote to her at length, and their exchange of confidences, something that he had long missed, was resumed on both sides. In this instance, the cataclysm affecting a whole world had been unable to wreak destruction.

He was now deeply grateful for the straightforward form his life had assumed. He was professionally successful, the business was prospering, at home his children were slowly growing from delicate, flower-like infancy to playful, talkative little creatures who regarded him with affection and kept him amused in the evening. And all that was left of the past, of the fiery blaze of his youth which had painfully consumed his days and nights, was a certain glow, the good, quiet light of friendship, making no demands and in no way dangerous. So two years later, when an American firm asked him to negotiate on its behalf for chemical patents in Berlin, it was a perfectly natural idea for him to think of greeting his lover of the past, now his friend, in person. As soon as he arrived in Berlin, his first request in his hotel was to be connected by telephone to her address in

Frankfurt; it seemed to him symbolic that nine years later the number was still the same. A good omen, he thought, nothing has changed. Then the telephone on the table rang boldly, and suddenly he was trembling with anticipation at the idea of hearing her voice again after so many years, a voice conjured up by that ringing, reaching this place across fields and meadows, above buildings and factory chimneys, close in spite of the many miles of years and water and earth between them. And no sooner had he given his name than he suddenly heard her cry out, in amazed astonishment, "Ludwig, is that really you?" It made its way to his ears first and then, dropping lower, to his heart, which was suddenly throbbing and full of blood. All at once something had set him alight. He had difficulty in speaking, and the light weight of the receiver dangled from his hand. The clear, startled note of surprise in her voice, her cry of joy ringing out, must have touched some hidden nerve in him, for he felt the blood humming in his temples and found it hard to make out what she was saying. And without consciously intending to do so, or knowing that he would, for it was as if someone were prompting him, he promised what he had never meant to say at all—he would be coming to Frankfurt the day after tomorrow. With that, his calm was destroyed. He feverishly did what he had come to do in Berlin, travelling swiftly around by motor car to get all the negotiations successfully completed at high speed. And when, on waking next morning, he remembered his dreams of the night just past, he knew that for the first time in years—the first time for four years—he had dreamed of her again.

Two days later, as he approached her house in the morning after a freezing night, having sent a telegram to announce his arrival, he suddenly thought, looking down at his own feet: this is not the way I walk, not the way I walk back across the ocean, going straight ahead with a confident, determined stride. Why am I walking like the shy, diffident twenty-three-year-old of the old days, anxiously dusting down his shabby coat again and again with shaking fingers, putting on his new gloves before ringing the doorbell? Why is my heart suddenly beating so fast, why do I feel self-conscious? In the old days I had secret presentiments of whatever was waiting to pounce on me beyond that copper-embossed door, and whether it would be good or bad. But why do I bow my head now, why does my rising uneasiness do away with all my firmness and certainty? He tried to remember who he was now, but in vain; he thought of his wife, his children, his house, his company, the foreign land where he lived. But all of that had faded, as if carried away by a ghostly mist; he felt alone, a petitioner once more, like the clumsy boy of the past in her presence. And the shaking hand that he now placed on the metal door handle was hot.

But as soon as he was inside the house that sense of being a stranger was gone, for the old manservant, now thin and desiccated, almost had tears in his eyes. "Doctor, it's you!" he kept faltering, with a sob in his voice. He was much moved. Odysseus, he thought, the household dogs recognize you, will the mistress of the house know you again too? But she was already opening the inner door, and came towards him with her hands held out. For a moment, as their hands joined, they looked at each other. It was a brief yet magically satisfying moment of comparison, examination, assessment, ardent memory and diffident delight, a moment when they happily exchanged covert glances again. Only then was the question resolved in a smile, and their glances became a familiar greeting. Yes, she was still the same, a little older, to be sure, on the left-hand side of her head silver threads ran through her hair, which she still wore parted in the middle, that glint of silver made her mild, friendly expression a little graver and more composed than before, and he felt the thirst of endless years quenched as he drank in the voice that now spoke to him, so intimate with its soft touch of regional accent. "Oh," she said, "how nice of you to come."

The sound was as pure and free as a tuning fork striking exactly the right note, and it set the tone for their entire conversation. Questions and anecdotes passed back and forth, like a pianist's right and left hands moving over the keyboard, clear and musical as they responded to one another. All the pent-up, smouldering awkwardness was dispersed by her presence and her first words. As long as she spoke, every thought obeyed her. But as soon as she fell silent, her eyelids lowered in thought, veiling her eyes, a question shot through his mind as swiftly as a shadow: "Aren't those the lips

I kissed?" And when she was called away to the telephone, leaving him alone in the room for a moment, the past came pressing stormily in on him from all sides. As long as her lucid presence ruled, that uncertain voice inside him had been subdued, but now every chair, every picture spoke to him, almost inaudibly whispering quiet words heard by him alone. I lived in this house, he could not help thinking, something of me lingers here, something of those years, the whole of me is not yet at home across the ocean, and I still do not live entirely in my own world. Then she came back into the room, cheerful as ever, and once again such ideas retreated into the background. "You will stay to lunch, won't you, Ludwig?" she said, taking it for granted. And he did stay, he stayed all day, and in conversation they looked back together at the past years. Only now that he was speaking of them did they truly seem real to him. And when he finally left, kissing her gentle maternal hand, and the door had closed behind him, he felt as if he had never been away.

That night, however, alone in the strange hotel room, with only the ticking of the clock beside him and his heart beating even harder in his breast, that sense of peace and calm was gone. He couldn't sleep, he rose, put on the light, switched it off again and lay there awake. He kept thinking of her lips, and how he had known them in a way very different from today's gently conversing familiarity. And suddenly he knew that all the casual talk between them had been pretence, that there was something still unrelieved and unresolved in their relationship, and the friendliness was merely an artificial mask over a nervous face, fitfully working in the throes of restless passion. He had imagined another kind of reunion with her for too long, on too many nights by the camp fire in his hut beyond the seas, for too many years and too many days—he had envisaged the two of them falling into each other's arms in a burning embrace, the final surrender, a dress slipping to the ground—he had imagined it too long for this friendliness, this courteous talk as they sounded each other out to ring entirely true. Actor and actress, he said to himself, we are both putting on a performance but neither of us is deceived. She is surely sleeping as little as I am tonight, he thought.

And when he went to see her next morning, she must have seen his loss of self-control and noticed his agitation and the evasive expression on his face at once, for the first thing she herself said was confused, and even later she could not find her way back to yesterday's easy, composed tone. Today their conversation was a matter of fits and starts, with pauses and awkward moments that had to be overcome with a forceful effort. Something or other stood between them, and questions and answers, invisibly coming up against it, ran into a dead end like bats flying into a wall. They both felt that they were skirting some other subject as they talked, and finally the conversation died down, reeling from this cautious circling of their words. He realized it in time and, when she invited him to stay for lunch again, invented an urgent appointment in the city.

She said she was very sorry, and indeed the shy warmth of her heart did now venture back into her voice. But she did not seriously try to keep him there. As she accompanied him out, their eyes nervously avoided each other. Something was crackling along their nerves, again and again conversation stumbled over the invisible obstacle that went with them from room to room, from word to word, and that now, growing stronger, took their breath away. So it was a relief when he was at the door, his coat already on. But all of a sudden, making up his mind, he turned back. "In fact there *is* something else I wanted to ask you before I go."

"You want to ask me something? By all means!" she smiled, radiant once again with the joy of being able to fulfil a wish of his.

"It may be foolish," he said, his glance diffident, "but I know that you'll understand. I would very much like to see my room again, the room where I lived for two years. All this time I've been down in the reception rooms that you keep for visitors, and if I leave like this, you see, I wouldn't feel I had been in my former home. As a man grows older he goes in search of his own youth, taking silly pleasure in little memories."

"You, grow older, Ludwig?" she replied almost light-heartedly. "I never thought you were so vain! Look at me, look at this grey streak in my hair. You're only a boy by comparison with me, and you talk of growing older already.

You must allow me to take precedence there! But how forgetful of me not to have taken you straight to your room, for that's what it still is. You will find nothing changed; nothing ever changes in this house."

"I hope that includes you," he said, trying to make a joke of it, but when she looked at him his expression instinctively changed to one of tender warmth.

She blushed slightly. "People may grow old, but they remain the same."

They went up to his old room. Even as they entered it there was a slight awkwardness, for she stood aside after opening the door to let him in, and as each of them courteously drew back at the same time to make way for the other, their shoulders briefly collided in the doorway. Both instinctively retreated, but even this fleeting physical contact was enough to embarrass them. She said nothing, but was overcome by a paralysing self-consciousness which was doubly perceptible in the silent, empty room. Nervously, she hurried over to the cords at the windows and pulled up the curtains, to let more light fall on the dark furnishings that seemed to be crouching there. But no sooner had bright light come suddenly rushing in than it was as if all those items of furniture suddenly had eyes and were stirring restlessly in alarm. Everything stood out in a significant way, speaking urgently of some memory. Here was the wardrobe that her attentive hand had always secretly kept in order for him, there were the bookshelves to which an addition was made when he had uttered a fleeting wish, there—speaking in yet sultrier tones—was the bed, where countless dreams of her, he knew, lay hidden under the bedspread. There in the corner—and this memory was burning hot as it came back to his mind—there was the ottoman where she had freed herself from him that last time. Inflamed by the passion now rekindled and blazing up, he saw signs and messages everywhere, left there by the woman now standing beside him, quietly breathing, compellingly strange, her eyes turned away and inscrutable. And the dense silence of the years, lying heavily as if slumped in the room, took alarm at their human presence and now assumed powerful proportions, settling on their lungs and troubled hearts like the blast of an explosion. Something had to be said, something must overcome that

silence to keep it from overwhelming them—
they both felt it. It was she, suddenly turning,
who broke the silence.

"Everything is just as it used to be, don't
you think?" she began, determined to say
something innocent and casual, although her
voice was husky and shook a little. However he
did not echo her friendly, conversational tone,
but gritted his teeth.

"Oh yes, everything." Sudden inner rage
forced the words abruptly and bitterly out
of his mouth. "Everything is as it used to be
except for us, except for us!"

The words cut into her. Alarmed, she turned
again.

"What do you mean, Ludwig?" But she did
not meet his gaze, for his eyes were not seeking
hers now but staring, silent and blazing, at
her lips, the lips he had not touched for so
many years, although once, moist on the
inside like a fruit, they had burned against
his own burning lips. In her embarrassment
she understood the sensuality of his gaze,
and a blush covered her face, mysteriously
rejuvenating her, so that she looked to him
just as she had looked in this same room when

he was about to leave. Once again she tried to fend off that dangerous gaze drawing her in, intentionally misunderstanding what could not be mistaken.

"What do you mean, Ludwig?" she repeated, but it was more of a plea for him not to tell her than a question requiring an answer.

Then, with a firm, determined look, he fixed his eyes on hers with masculine strength. "You pretend not to understand me, but I know you do. Do you remember this room—and do you remember what you promised me here … when I came back?"

Her shoulders were shaking as she still tried to fend him off. "No, don't say it, Ludwig … this is all old history, let's not touch on it. Where are those times now?"

"In us," he replied firmly, "in what we want. I have waited nine years, keeping grimly silent, but I haven't forgotten. And I am asking you, do you still remember?"

"Yes." She looked at him more steadily now. "I have not forgotten either."

"And will you—" he had to take a deep breath, to give force to what he as about to say—"will you keep your promise?"

The colour came to her face again, surging up to her hairline. She moved towards him, as if to placate him. "Ludwig, do think! You said you haven't forgotten anything—so don't forget, I am almost an old woman now. When a woman's hair turns grey she has no more to wish for, no more to give. I beg you, let the past rest."

But a great desire now came over him to be hard and determined. "You are trying to avoid me," he said inexorably, "but I have waited too long. I ask you, do you remember your promise?"

Her voice faltered with every word she spoke. "Why do you ask me? There's no point in my saying this to you now, now that it's all too late. But if you insist, I will answer you. I could never have denied you anything, I was always yours from the day when I first met you."

He looked at her—how honest she was even in her confusion, how truthful and straightforward, showing no cowardice, making no excuses, his steadfast beloved, always the same, preserving her dignity so wonderfully at every moment, both reserved and candid. Instinctively he stepped towards her, but as soon as she saw his impetuous movement she warded him off.

"Come along now, Ludwig, come—let's not stay here, let's go downstairs. It is midday, the maid could come looking for me at any moment. We mustn't stay here any longer."

And so irresistibly did her own strength dominate his will that, just as in the past, he obeyed her without a word. They went down to the reception rooms, through the front hall and to the door without another word, without exchanging a glance. At the door, he suddenly turned to her.

"I can't say any more to you now, forgive me. I will write to you."

She smiled at him gratefully. "Yes, do write to me, Ludwig, that will be better."

And no sooner was he back in his hotel room than he sat down at the desk and wrote her a long letter, compulsively carried along by his suddenly thwarted passion from word to word, from page to page. This was his last day in Germany for months, he wrote, for years, perhaps for ever, and he would not, could not leave her like this, pretending to make cool conversation, forced into the mendacity of correct social behaviour. He wanted to, he must talk to her once more, away from the house, away from fears and

memories and the oppressive, inhibiting, watch-
ful atmosphere of its rooms. So he was asking
whether she would take the evening train with
him to Heidelberg, where they had both once
been for a brief visit a decade ago when they were
still strangers to one another, yet already feeling
a presentiment of intimacy. Today, however, it
would be to say goodbye, a last goodbye, it was
what he still most profoundly desired. He was
asking her to give him this one evening, this night.
He hastily sealed the letter and sent it over to her
house by messenger. In quarter-of-an-hour the
messenger was back, bringing a small envelope
sealed with yellow wax. His hand trembled as he
tore it open. There was only a note inside it, a
few words in her firm, determined handwriting,
set down on the paper in haste, yet in her forceful
handwriting:

"What you ask is folly, but I never could, I
never will deny you anything. I will come."

The train slowed down as they passed the
flickering lights of a station. Instinctively the
dreamer's gaze moved away from introspection
to look outside himself, again seeking tenderly

for the figure of his dream in the alternating light and shade. Yes, there she was, ever faithful, always silently loving, she had come with him, to him—again and again he savoured her physical presence. And as if something in her had sensed his questing glance, feeling that shyly caressing touch from afar, she sat up straight now and looked out of the window beyond which the vague outlines of the landscape, wet in the spring darkness, slipped past like glittering water.

"We should be arriving soon," she said as if to herself.

"Yes," he said, sighing deeply, "it has taken so long."

He himself did not know whether, by those words impatiently uttered, he meant the train journey or all the long years leading up to this hour—a confused sense of mingled dream and reality surged through him. He felt only that beneath him the rattling wheels were rolling on towards something, towards some moment that, now in a strangely muted mood, he could not clarify in his mind. No, he would not think of that, he would let an invisible power carry him on as it willed, with his limbs relaxed, towards something mysterious. He felt a kind of bridal expectation, sweet and sensuous yet vaguely mingled with anticipatory fear of its own fulfilment, with the mysterious shiver felt when something endlessly desired suddenly comes physically close to the astonished heart. But he must not think that out to the end now, he must not want anything, desire anything, he must simply stay like this, carried on into the unknown as if in a dream, carried on by a strange torrent, without physical sensation and yet still feeling, desiring yet achieving nothing, moving on into his fate and back into himself. Oh, to stay like this for hours longer, for an eternity, in this continuous twilight, surrounded by dreams—but already, like a faint fear, the thought came into his mind that this could soon be over.

Here and there, in all directions, electric sparks of light were flickering on in the valley like fireflies, brighter and brighter as they blinked past. Street lamps closed together in straight double rows, the tracks were rattling by, and already a pale dome of brighter vapour was emerging from the darkness.

"Heidelberg," said one of the legal gentlemen to his companions. All three picked up their bulging briefcases and hurried out of the compartment so as to reach the carriage door as soon as possible. The wheels, with brakes applied to them, were now jolting and rattling into the station. There was an abrupt, bone-shaking jerk, the train's speed slackened, and the wheels squealed only once more, like a tortured animal. For a second the two of them sat alone, facing each other, as if startled by the sudden onset of reality.

"Are we there already?" She sounded almost alarmed.

"Yes," he replied, and stood up. "Can I help you?" She refused with a gesture and went quickly ahead. But on the step down from the carriage she hesitated, her foot faltering for a moment as if about to step down into ice-cold water. Then she pulled herself together, and he followed in silence. And then they stood on the platform side by side for a moment, helpless with awkward emotion, like strangers, and the small suitcase weighed heavy as it dangled from his hand. Suddenly the engine beside them, snorting again, let off steam shrilly. She started, and then looked at him, her face pale, her eyes unsure and bewildered.

92

"What is it?" he asked.

"A pity it's over; it was so pleasant, just riding along like that. I could have gone on for hours and hours."

He said nothing. He had been thinking just the same at that moment. But now it *was* over, and something had to happen.

"Shall we go?" he cautiously asked.

"Yes, let's go," she murmured barely audibly. None the less, they still stood there side by side, as if some spring inside them had broken. Only then—and he forgot to take her arm—did they turn undecidedly away towards the station exit.

They left the station, but no sooner were they out of the door than stormy noise met their ears, drums rattling, the shrill sound of pipes— it was a patriotic demonstration of veterans' associations and students in support of the Fatherland. Like walls on the move, marching in ranks four abreast, flags flying, men in military garb were goose-stepping along, feet thudding heavily on the ground, marching all in time like a single man, necks thrown stiffly back, the very image of powerful determination with mouths

93

open in song, one voice, one step, keeping time. In front marched generals, white-haired dignitaries bedecked with orders and flanked by companies of younger men, marching with athletic firmness, carrying huge banners held vertically erect and bearing death's heads, the swastika, the banners of the Reich waving in the wind, their broad chests thrust out, their heads braced as if to march against an enemy's batteries. They marched in a throng—they might have been propelled forward by a fist keeping time—all in geometrical order, preserving a distance as precise as if it had been drawn by compasses, keeping step, every nerve gravely tensed, a menacing expression on their faces, and every time a new rank—of veterans, of youth groups, of students—passed the raised platform where percussion instruments kept drumming out a steely rhythm on an invisible anvil, the many heads turned with military precision. With one accord they looked left, a movement running along the backs of all those necks, and the banners were raised as if on strings before the army commander who, stony-faced, was taking the salute of these civilians. Beardless boys, youths with the first down on their chins, faces etched with the lines of age, workers, students, soldiers or boys, they all looked exactly the same for that split second, with their harsh, determined, angry expressions, chins defiantly jutting, hands going to the hilts of invisible swords. And again and again, from troop to troop, the drumbeat hammered out, its monotony doubly inflaming feelings, keeping the marchers' backs straight, their eyes hard, forging war and vengeance by their invisible presence here in a peaceful square, under a sky with soft clouds sweetly passing over it.

"Madness," he exclaimed to himself, in astonishment, faltering. "Madness! What do they want? Once again, once again!"

War once again, war that had so recently shattered his whole life? With a strange shudder, he looked at those young faces, staring at the black mass on the move in ranks of four, like a square strip of film running, unrolling out of a narrow alley as if out of a dark box, and every face it showed was instantly rigid with bitter determination, a threat, a weapon. Why was this threat so noisily uttered on a mild June evening, hammered home in a gently dreaming city?

"What do they want? What do they want?"
The question still had him by the throat. Only
just now he had seen the world in bright, musical
clarity, with the light of love and tenderness
shining over it, he had been part of a melody
of kindness and trust. And suddenly the iron
steps of that marching throng were treading
everything down, men girding themselves for
the fray, men of a thousand different kinds,
shouting with a thousand voices, yet expressing
only one thing in their eyes and their onward
march, hate, hate, hate.

He instinctively took her arm so as to feel
something warm, love, passion, kindness,
sympathy, a soft, soothing sensation, yet the
drums broke through his inner silence, and
now that all the thousands of voices were
raised in what was unmistakably a war song,
now that the ground was shaking with feet
marching in time, the air exploding in sudden
jubilant hurrahs from the huge mob, he felt
as if something tender and sweet-sounding
inside him was crushed by the powerful, noisily
forceful drone of reality.

A slight movement at his side drew his
attention to her hand with its gloved fingers,

gently deterring his own from clenching so wildly into a fist. Then he turned his eyes, which had been fixed on the crowd—she was looking at him pleadingly, without words, he merely felt her gently compelling touch on his arm.

"Yes, let's go," he murmured, pulling himself together, hunching his shoulders as if to ward off something invisible, and he began forcing a way through the conveniently close-packed crowd of spectators, all staring as silently as he had been, spellbound, at the never-ending march past of these military legions. He did not know where he was going, he just wanted to get out of this tumultuous crowd, away from this square where all that was gentle in him, all dreams, were being ground down as if in a mortar by this pitiless rhythm. Just to get away, be alone with her, with this one woman, surrounded by the dark, under a roof, feeling her breath, able to look into her eyes at his leisure, unwatched, for the first time in ten years, to enjoy being alone with her. It was something he had promised himself in so many dreams, and now it was almost swept away by that swirling human mass marching and singing, a surging wave constantly breaking over itself. His nervous gaze went to the buildings, all with banners draped over their facades, but many of them had gold lettering proclaiming that they were business premises, and some were restaurants. All at once he felt the little suitcase pulling slightly at his hand, conveying a message—he longed to rest, to be at home somewhere, and alone! To buy a handful of silence and a few square metres of space! And as if in answer, the gleaming golden name of a hotel now leaped to the eye above a tall stone façade, and its glazed porch curved out to meet them. He was walking slowly, taking shallow breaths. Almost dazed, he stopped, and instinctively let go of her arm. "This is supposed to be a good hotel. It was recommended to me," he said untruthfully and awkwardly.

She flinched back in alarm, blood pouring into her pale face. He lips moved, trying to say something—perhaps the same words she had said ten years ago, that distressed, "Not now! Not here."

But then she saw his gaze turning to her, anxious, disturbed, nervous. And she bowed her head in silent consent, and followed him, with small and daunted steps, to the entrance.

In the reception area of the hotel a porter, wearing a brightly coloured cap and with the self-important air of a ship's captain at his lookout post, stood behind the desk that kept them at a distance. He did not move towards them as they hesitantly entered, merely cast a fleeting and disparaging look at them, taking in the small suitcase. He waited, and they had to approach him. He was now apparently busy again with the folio pages of the big register open before him. Only when the prospective guests were right in front of him did he raise cool eyes to inspect them objectively and severely. "Have you booked in with us, sir?" He then responded to the almost guilty negative by leafing through the register again. "I'm afraid we are fully booked. There was a big ceremony here today, the consecration of the flag—but," he added graciously, "I'll see what I can do."

Oh, to punch this sergeant-major with his braided uniform in the face, thought the humiliated man bitterly. A beggar again, a petitioner, an intruder for the first time in a decade. But by now the self-satisfied porter had finished his lengthy study of the register.

"Number twenty-seven has just fallen vacant, a double room, if you'd care to take that." What was there to do but to say, with a muted growl, a swift, "Yes, that will do," and his restless fingers took the key handed to him, impatient as he already was to have silent walls between himself and this man. Then, behind him, he heard the stern voice again: "Register here, please," and a rectangular form was place in front of him, with ten or twelve headings to boxes that must be filled in with title, name, age, place of origin, place of residence, all the intrusive questions that officialdom puts to living human beings. The distasteful task was quickly performed, pencil flying—only when he had to enter her surname, untruthfully uniting it in marriage with his (though once that had been his secret wish), did the light weight of the pencil shake clumsily in his hand. "Duration of stay, please," demanded the implacable doorman, running his eye over the completed form and pointing to the one box still empty. "One day," wrote the pencil angrily. In his agitation he felt his moist forehead and had to take off his hat, the air here in this strange place seemed so oppressive.

"First floor on the left," said a courteous waiter, swiftly coming up as the exhausted man turned aside. But he was looking around for her. All through this procedure she had been standing motionless, showing intense interest in a poster announcing a Schubert recital to be given by an unknown singer, but as she stood there, very still, a slight quiver kept passing over her shoulders like the wind blowing over a grassy meadow. He noticed, ashamed, how she was controlling her agitation by main force; why, he thought against his will, did I tear her away from her quiet home to bring her here? But now there was no going back. "Come on," he urged her quietly. Without showing him her face, she moved away from the poster that meant nothing to them and went ahead up the stairs, slowly and treading heavily, with difficulty—like an old woman, he involuntarily reflected.

That thought lasted for a mere second as she made her way up the few steps, with her hand on the banister rail, and he immediately banished the ugly idea. But something cold and hurtful remained in his mind, replacing the thought he had so forcibly dismissed from it.

At last they were upstairs in the corridor—
those two silent minutes had been an eternity.
A door stood open. It was the door of their
room, and the chambermaid was still busy with
broom and duster in it. "I'll soon be finished,"
she excused herself. "The room's only this
moment been vacated, but sir and madam can
come in, I'll just fetch clean sheets."

They went in. The air in the closed room was
musty and sweetish, smelling of olive soap and
cold cigarette smoke. Somewhere the unseen
trace of other guests still lingered.

Boldly, perhaps still warm from human
bodies, the unmade double bed bore visible
witness to the point and purpose of this room.
He was nauseated by its explicit meaning, and
instinctively went to the window and opened it.
Soft damp air, mingled with the muted noise
of the street, drifted slowly in past the gently
fluttering curtains. He stayed there at the open
window, looking out intently at the now dark
rooftops. How ugly this room was, how shaming
their presence here seemed, how disappointing
was this moment when they were together, a
moment longed for so much over the years—
but neither he nor she had wanted it to be so

sudden, to show itself in all its shameless nudity!
For the space of three, four, five breaths—he
counted them—he looked out, too cowardly to
speak first, but then he forced himself to do so.
No, no, this would not do, he said. And just as
he had known and feared in advance, she stood
in the middle of the room as if turned to stone
in her grey dustcoat, her arms hanging down as
if they had snapped, as if she were something
that did not belong here and had entered this
unpleasant room only by the accident of force
and chance. She had taken off her gloves,
obviously to put them down, but then she must
have felt revulsion against the idea of placing
them anywhere here, and so they dangled
empty from her fingers, like the husks of her
hands. Her gaze was fixed, her eyes veiled, but
when he turned they looked at him with a plea
in them. He understood. "Why don't we—"
and his voice stumbled over the breath he was
expelling—"why don't we go for a little walk?
It's so gloomy in here."

"Yes, yes!" She uttered the word as if liberating
it, letting fear off the chain. And already her
hand was reaching for the door handle. He
followed her more slowly, and saw her shoulders

shaking like the flanks of an animal when it has just escaped the clutch of deadly claws.

The street was waiting, warm and crowded. In the wake of the ceremonial rally, the human current was still restless, so they turned off into quieter streets, finding the path through the woods that had taken them up to the castle on an excursion ten years ago. "It was a Sunday, do your remember?" he said, instinctively speaking in a loud voice, and she, obviously calling the same memory to mind, replied quietly, "I haven't forgotten anything I did with you. Otto had his school friend with him, and they hurried on ahead so fast that we almost lost them in the woods. I called for him, telling him to come back, and I didn't do it willingly, because I so much wanted to be alone with you. But we were still strangers to each other at that time."

"And today too," he said, trying to make a joke of it. But she did not reply. I ought not to have said that, he felt vaguely; what makes me keep comparing the past with the present? But why can't I say anything right to her today? The past always comes between us, the time that has gone by.

So they climbed the rising slope of the road in silence. The houses below them were already huddling close together in the faint light, the curving river showed more clearly in the twilight of the valley, while here the trees rustled and darkness fell over them. No one came towards them, only their own shadows went ahead in silence. And whenever a lamp by the roadside cast its light on them at an angle, the shadows ahead merged as if embracing, stretching, longing for one another, two bodies in one form, parting again only to embrace once more, while they themselves walked on, tired and apart from each other. As if spellbound, he watched this strange game, that escape and recapture and separation again of the soulless figures, shadowy bodies that were only the reflection of their own. With a kind of sick curiosity he saw the flight and merging of those insubstantial figures, and as he watched the black, flowing, fleeting image before him, he almost forgot the living woman at his side. He was not thinking clearly of anything, yet he felt vaguely that this furtive game was a warning of something that lay deep as a well within him, but was now insistently rising, like the bucket dipped into the well menacingly reaching the surface. What was it? He strained every sense. What was the shadow play here in the sleeping woods telling him? There must be words in it, a situation, something he had experienced, heard, felt, something hidden in a melody, a deeply buried memory that he had not touched for many years.

And suddenly it came to him, a lightning flash in the darkness of oblivion—yes, words, a poem that she had once read aloud to him in the drawing room in the evening. A French poem, he still knew the words, and as if blown to him by a hot wind they were suddenly rising to his lips; he heard those forgotten lines from a poem in another language spoken, over a space of ten years, in her voice:

Dans le vieux parc solitaire et glacé
Deux spectres cherchent le passé.

And as soon as those lines lit up in his memory, an image joined them at magical speed—the lamp with its golden light in the darkened drawing room where she had read Verlaine's poem to him one evening. He saw her in the shadow cast by the lamp, sitting both near to him and far away, beloved and out of reach, he suddenly felt his own heart of those days hammering with excitement to hear her voice coming to him on the musical wave of the words, hearing her say the words of the poem—although only in the poem—words that spoke of love and longing, in a foreign language and meant for a stranger, yet it was intoxicating to hear them in that voice, her voice. He wondered how he could have forgotten it all these years, that poem, that evening when they had been on their own in the house, confused because they were alone, taking flight from the dangers of conversation into the easier terrain of books, where a confession of more intimate feelings sometimes showed clearly through the words and the melody, flashing like light in the bushes, sparkling intangibly, yet comforting without any palpable presence. How could he have forgotten it for so long? But how was it that the forgotten poem had suddenly surfaced again? Involuntarily, he spoke the lines aloud, translating them:

In the old park, in ice and snow caught fast
Two spectres walk, still searching for the past.

And no sooner had he said it than she understood, and placed the room-key, heavy and shining, in his hand, so abruptly did that one sharply outlined, bright association plucked from the sleeping depths of memory come to the surface. The shadows there on the path had touched and woken her own words, and more besides. With a shiver running down his spine, he suddenly felt the full truth and sense of them. Had not those spectres searching for their past been muted questions, asked of a time that was no longer real, mere shadows wanting to come back to life but unable to do so now? Neither she nor he was the same any more, yet they were searching for each other in a vain effort, fleeing one another, persisting in disembodied, powerless efforts like those black spectres at their feet.

Unconsciously, he must have groaned aloud, for she turned. "What's the matter, Ludwig? What are you thinking of?"

But he merely dismissed it, saying, "Nothing, nothing!" And he listened yet more intently to what was within him, to the past, to see whether that voice of memory truly foretelling the future would not speak to him again, revealing the present to him as well as the past.

TRANSLATOR'S AFTERWORD

T HIS NOVELLA BY STEFAN ZWEIG has an inter-
esting and indeed complex publishing history. For a number of the details below I am
indebted to the preface by the French translator Baptiste Touverey to the recent French edition, published in 2008 by Editions Grasset, and
in particular to Professor Rüdiger Görner of
Queen Mary, University of London, who has
most kindly shared his comprehensive knowledge of Zweig and his works with me.

In France, the novella has aroused much
interest as being previously unpublished,
which is strictly true of its being previously
unpublished in French, and indeed to the best
of my knowledge in English. Although it was
published in German after its full text came
to light in the 1970s, and was then included in
the standard German editions of the complete
works of Zweig, that was at a time when, after

Zweig's death thirty years earlier, interest in his works had waned in the English-speaking countries.

However, he had begun to write the story in the 1920s, probably around 1924 while he was also working on an essay on the poet Hölderlin. The Hölderlin essay was later included, with similar studies of Friedrich Nietzsche and Heinrich von Kleist, in a book entitled *Der Kampf mit dem Dämon* [Battle with the Demon], and dedicated to Sigmund Freud. All three of Zweig's subjects in this work, notable literary figures in the late eighteenth century and the nineteenth century in Germany, suffered from some degree of mental disturbance (severe in the first two, sufficient in Kleist's case to drive him to kill himself in a suicide pact). Zweig took a great interest in what was, in his day, the comparatively new field of psychology, so the dedication to Freud comes as no surprise. Some of the writers working in the Vienna of Freud's prime themselves had a medical training—Arthur Schnitzler, for instance, whose literary works Freud himself praised for their psychological insight, and Kafka's friend Ernst Weiss. Stefan Zweig was not one of these

literary physicians, but his psychological insight
as mirrored in his fiction is in no way inferior
to Schnitzler's. An interest in exploring the
interaction of mind, heart and body seems to
have been in the literary air of Vienna at the
time.

As a prolific writer in a number of genres,
including fiction, novellas, plays, biography
and literary criticism, Zweig often worked on
more than one project at the same time. The
date of 1924 for his embarking on the present
novella would mean that he was not looking
back very far in time for the latter part of his
story, which concludes three years after the
end of the First World War. Although Zweig
was not a writer to include elements of his
own life story in his fiction—it is otherwise
with his ideas, for instance his strongly held
pacifist views, which are to the fore here and in
several of his other novellas—it is possible to
imagine a slight, although not close, reflection
of his personal situation in the plot of the
novella. Zweig and the writer Friederike von
Winternitz, who was to be his first wife, met
in 1912 when she was married with children,
and it was not until the end of the Great War

that she finally divorced her husband and, in 1920, married Zweig. They were not, however, divided like the couple in this story by oceans and continents for the duration of the war. Although they ultimately divorced in 1938, they continued to correspond on friendly terms until Zweig's death in 1942.

Zweig went on with the story in the summer of 1925, while he was also working on two other novellas, *Twenty-Four Hours in the Life of a Woman* and *Downfall of a Heart*, and a part of it was published in Vienna in 1929 under the title *Fragment of a Novella*, in an anthology of works by the Austrian National Association of Creative Artists. He must have continued working on it in the 1930s—Rüdiger Görner surmises that he was not entirely happy with the fragment published in 1929—and later Knut Beck, editor at S Fischer Verlag, the publisher of the standard editions of Zweig's work in German, found a typescript of the complete novella in the archives of Atrium Press, London, with handwritten corrections and changes by Zweig himself. He had written in a title corresponding to that used in the new French edition, *Le Voyage dans le passé* [*Journey into the Past*], and although he then crossed it out, the French publisher and translator decided to retain it. We have settled on a similar phrasing in English, one that tells the reader a little more about the content of the novella than its now standard German title, *Widerstand der Wirklichkeit* [Resistance to Reality].

To me it is fascinating to know that this novella stems originally from the same period as Zweig's *Twenty-Four Hours in the Life of a Woman*, also a Pushkin Press title, because in translation one comes to know a work, or in this case two works, very well indeed. The same highly charged emotional atmosphere and delicately perceptive understanding of psychological nuances pervade both novellas, with the difference that *Twenty-Four Hours*, by definition, covers the short period of time specified in the title, whereas *Journey into the Past* has a narrative stretching over nine years, because of the disruption to the lives of the story's protagonists by the Great War of 1914–18 and subsequent events. The time span could scarcely be more different, yet the sense of strong emotional tension is strikingly similar in both novellas. Incidentally, Zweig's meticulous but at the same time condensed style makes him a challenge to translate, although an enjoyable challenge. You read him in the original, and on the surface everything is limpid, lucid; then you start translating him, and you have to think hard about what exactly lies below the wording of every sentence.

Short as the final version of the novella is, the Great War looms very large in it, and not just as a plot device. Zweig was a pacifist, and his fiction of this period reflects his strong feelings—another novella to which the subject is central is his *Compulsion*. For much of the Great War, having been declared unfit for military service anyway, Zweig worked in the archives of the Austrian War Office, but his anti-war opinions became ever more pronounced—he was a close friend of the French writer Romain Rolland, also a pacifist—and in 1917 he took the opportunity of moving to neutral Switzerland until the war was over. *Journey into the Past* expresses the sense of horrified helplessness felt by people who feel no bellicose patriotism whatsoever, but are overtaken by armed conflict. The personal lives of the protagonist Ludwig and other European expatriates in Mexico, where he finds himself when war breaks out in 1914, are cast into turmoil when they are cut off from their homes, unable even to communicate in letters any more. Zweig describes the moment when news of the declaration of war reaches him as "the disastrous day that pitilessly tore up not only my calendar but, with total indifference, the lives and thoughts of millions, leaving them in shreds". As an added illustration of the sudden reversal of ordinary circumstances, Ludwig finds that "the British consul, a friend of his … indicated with a cautious note of warning in his voice that he personally was obliged to keep an eye on all his movements from now on".

And not only does the First World War figure prominently, so at the very end does the looming shadow of the Second World War. Ludwig has persuaded his former lover to spend a night in Heidelberg with him, but when they arrive at the railway station his mood of nostalgic passion and the quiet peace of the town alike are shattered by a nationalist demonstration. It is useful to remember here that almost as soon as the First War was over, right-wing opinion in Germany, where the terms of the Versailles Treaty were widely and bitterly resented, began to express itself in such demonstrations as the one that shocks Ludwig so much. The Versailles Treaty had placed strict constraints on the numbers of the German army, and the reader will notice that Zweig specifically speaks of the demonstrators as 'civilians'. But directly after the war, volunteer bodies known as Freikorps began to form, and these groups amounted to private armies. Many were then absorbed into Adolf Hitler's *Sturmabteilung* (Storm Section, infamous in history as the brownshirts or SA). The SA acted as bodyguards for the leaders of what became known in 1920 as the National Socialist German Workers' Party, the Nazi Party, formed on the basis of the immediate post-war German Workers' Party.

The reader will find also find mention of "banners of the Reich" in the text, and although we think of the period from the end of the Great War until 1933 as the Weimar Republic—not an official name—and government was indeed on republican principles, the term *Reich* remained in use as a term for its governing institutions. It was not until 1933 that Hitler, by then a popular demagogue, became Chancellor of Germany, proclaimed a Third Reich and ensured the passing of the Enabling Act which, in effect, made the country a dictatorship. As Stefan Zweig's account shows, he had been building up support for the Nazi Party throughout the 1920s. (One term, *Jungvolk*, often and correctly translated as 'Hitler Youth', I have left as 'youth groups', because the name Hitler Youth was not officially adopted until 1926, and we do not seem to have reached that point yet in the chronology of the story.) Protracted as Hitler's rise to power was, however, coming events cast a long shadow before them, and Zweig's protagonist in *Journey into the Past*, having felt the effects on his personal life of the First World War, is horrified to think of the prospect of war again.

Before it came, as he had known it would, Zweig went into exile, as so many other Jewish writers in Germany and Austria did, including his friend Joseph Roth—famous and distinguished as Sigmund Freud was, he too had to leave for England to die of cancer there. In an unprecedented act of vandalism, the books of 'subversive Jewish writers' were burned in university cities the length and breadth of Germany in May 1933; so willingly had the

119

right-wing student organizations embraced the ideas of Hitler and his propaganda minister Goebbels that they themselves organized the book-burnings. Still in Austria at the time, Zweig wrote to Romain Rolland: "My dear friend, I reply to you today, on May the 10th … when my books burn on the bonfire in Berlin outside the University, where I once spoke about you to an audience of a thousand." Five months later he left his house in Salzburg, never to return.

England was Zweig's own first country of exile, and he then went to the United States and finally to Brazil. Here, early in 1942, he and his second wife Lotte killed themselves in a suicide pact. It has been suggested that he had been cast into despair by military successes in the Far East on the part of Japan, which with Italy was Germany's main ally in the Second World War, but a year before Zweig's suicide the United States had entered the war on the side of the Allies, and it was beginning to be clear (if not just yet to the Germans themselves), that Hitler's promises of a final victory were empty rhetoric, and Nazi Germany would ultimately lose. Many people now surmise, for instance Clive James in his clear and useful essay on

Zweig as a cultural cosmopolitan, that he despaired because the old, civilized world of a pan-European culture, in which he had been so much at home, seemed lost already in a time of new barbarism, and while the Nazis might lose the war itself, they had already, as James puts it, "won the war that mattered".

Zweig's last work of fiction was the famous *Schachnovelle*, commonly known by the familiar English title of *The Royal Game*—the royal game, or game of kings, of course being chess. It is a sad irony that his protagonist here, Dr B, is a man who has survived solitary confinement in Nazi captivity by occupying his mind with chess problems, although his experience leaves him profoundly damaged. Dying by his own hand at the age of sixty, Zweig himself might well have written much worth reading if he too had survived.

Stefan Zweig was indeed not just an Austrian but a truly European writer, a fact very evident in his memoir of his life and times, *The World of Yesterday*. Whether or not the idea suggested above was the reason for his suicide, everything was not lost after all. Although Germany and Austria under the Nazis had, by means of anti-Semitic persecution culminating in the Holocaust, deliberately deprived themselves of the great contribution made by their Jewish citizens to the art, music and literature of their countries, a cultural revival accompanied the economic miracle. The exiled writers like Roth and Zweig—with of course such cultural figures as Thomas Mann who, although not Jewish, left Nazi Germany to go into voluntary exile—now receive their due.

At the time of writing this note, I have recently read a long and very fine novel by Uwe Tellkamp, *Der Turm* [*The Tower*], published by Suhrkamp and winner of the 2008 German Book Prize for fiction, in which we hear how deeply its central character, a clever teenager in Dresden in the 1980s when the former East German Republic was inexorably crumbling, is impressed by Zweig's *The World of Yesterday*. Brought up in East Germany, where children in his time are obliged, right to the rapidly approaching end in the 1980s, to trot out Communist Party slogans, the boy is amazed to read the memoir and realize that, on Zweig's evidence, there was a time before the Second World War and the communist regimes in Eastern

Europe when cultural cosmopolitanism prevailed throughout the continent. It is easy to concur with the young man's view of Stefan Zweig as the embodiment of that civilized idea.

Two further brief notes on the translation of the novella—first, we learn early on that the husband of the married woman with whom Ludwig falls in love is a *Geheimrat*. This title always gives an English translator difficulty. Literally it means Privy Councillor, and once it really did mean that, but by the early twentieth century it had come to be purely honorific, denoting nothing much except that a man had distinguished himself in his own sphere of life, in the case of Councillor G as an industrialist and chemist. I have added the briefest of explanations on the first occurrence of the term, and then referred to him as 'the Councillor'. *Geheimrat* as an honorary title went out of use after the Great War. And second, at the very end of the novella a nostalgic memory surfaces in Ludwig's mind; he recollects his beloved once reading a poem by Verlaine aloud to him, *Colloque sentimental*. Zweig has his protagonist reciting a couplet from this poem first in French—*Dans le vieux parc solitaire et glacé/ Deux spectres cherchent le passé*, and then translating it into German (which I have translated into English). In fact Zweig's text merges the second line of the first couplet in the French original—*Deux formes ont tout à l'heure passé*—with the second line of the third couplet: *Deux spectres ont évoqué le passé.* I have left it exactly as Zweig had it, since, whether intentionally or subliminally, he was adapting Verlaine's words to the idea that he wanted of two spectres in search of the past.

ANTHEA BELL 2009

Pushkin Press

Pushkin Press was founded in 1997, and publishes novels, essays, memoirs, children's books—everything from timeless classics to the urgent and contemporary.

Our books represent exciting, high-quality writing from around the world: we publish some of the twentieth century's most widely acclaimed, brilliant authors such as Stefan Zweig, Marcel Aymé, Antal Szerb, Paul Morand and Yasushi Inoue, as well as compelling and award-winning contemporary writers, including Andrés Neuman, Edith Pearlman and Ryu Murakami.

Pushkin Press publishes the world's best stories, to be read and read again.

*